SEARCHING FOR GOREN

THE NINE LIVES OF GABRIELLE: FOR THREE SHE PLAYS - BOOK 2

LAURA MARIANI

The
PEOPLE
ALCHEMIST

CONTENTS

ABOUT THE AUTHOR

Laura Mariani is an Author, Speaker and Entrepreneur.

She started her consulting business after a successful career as Senior HR Director within global brands in FMCG, Retail, Media and Pharma.

Laura is incredibly passionate about helping other women to break through barriers limiting their personal and/or professional fulfilment. Her best selling nonfiction *STOP IT! It is all in your head* and the *THINK, LOOK & ACT THE PART* series have been described as success and transformation 101.

She is a Fellow of the Chartered Institute of Personnel & Development (FCIPD), Fellow of the Australian Human Resources Institute (FAHRI), Fellow of the Institute of Leadership & Management (FInstLM), Member of the Society of Human Resources Management (SHRM) and Member of the Change Institute.

She is based in London, England with a strong penchant for travel and visiting new places. She is a food lover, ballet fanatic, passionate about music, art, theatre. She likes painting and drawing (for self-expression not selling but hey, you never know…), tennis, rugby, and of course fashion (the Pope is Catholic after all).

www.thepeoplealchemist.com
@PeopleAlchemist
instagram.com/lauramariani_author

NEW FICTION BY LAURA MARIANI

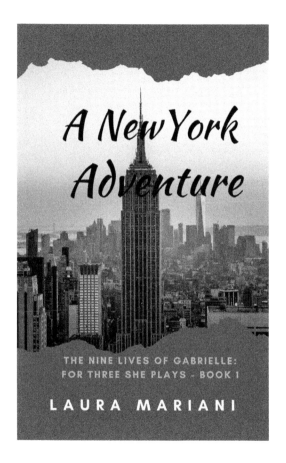

A New York Adventure

THE NINE LIVES OF GABRIELLE:
FOR THREE SHE PLAYS - BOOK 1

LAURA MARIANI

GABRIELLE STORY CONTINUE ...

THE NINE LIVES OF GABRIELLE:
FOR THREE SHE PLAYS - BOOK 3

Tasting
Freedom

LAURA MARIANI

NEW NON-FICTION BY LAURA MARIANI

ALSO BY LAURA MARIANI

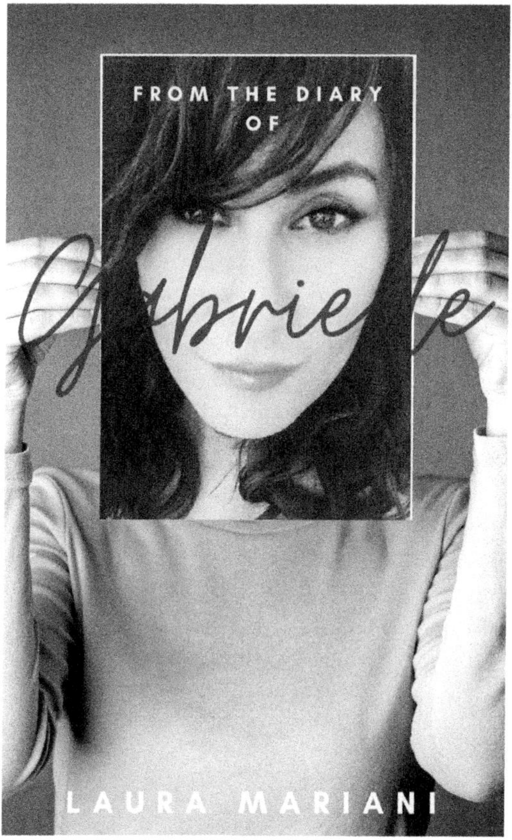
FROM THE DIARY
OF
Gabrielle
LAURA MARIANI

Non-Fiction

STOP IT! It is all in your head

The RULE BOOK to Smash The infamous glass ceiling - For women & young women everywhere - personal transformation & success 101.

The Think, Look & Act The Part Series.

Think The Part

Upgrade your consciousness and mind-set. Make winning a key part of your life and business.

Look The Part

Upgrade your personal brand. Make presenting your unique Best Self a key part of your life and business.

Act The Part

A personal coach to act in spite of fear, right here, right now.

More non-fiction books and courses are coming soon. For new releases, giveaways and pre-release specials check www. thepeoplealchemist.com

You can also buy my books and courses directly from me at www. payhip.com/LauraMariani

ThePeopleAlchemist Press publishes self help, inspirational and transformational books, resources and products to help #TheWomanAlchemist in every woman to change her life/ career and transmute any circumstance into gold, a bit like magic to **Unlock Ignite Transform.**

ISBN: 978-1-915501-04-2

Reality can be so much better than fantasy.
If you'd only let it.

PREFACE

What if we are always choosing people who don't allow intimacy?

Is it because, deep down, we don't want intimacy? Or are we afraid we'd lose ourselves entirely if we let ourselves be loved?

Committed to not committing.

SEARCHING FOR GOREN

"Io sono qui, e non mi pesa la lunga attesa. Io ti aspetto", said Mr Wonderful whilst looking at Gabrielle and kissing her gently on her forehead.

The singer was belting one of Madame Butterfly's most famous arias, Un bel dì, vedremo:

> *E non mi pesa*
> *La lunga attesa*
> *E uscito dalla folla cittadina*
> *Un uomo, un picciol punto*
> *S'avvia per la collina*
> *Chi sarà, chi sarà?*
> *E come sarà giunto*
> *Che dirà, che dirà?*

She smiled, not knowing what to say. Sometimes he could read her mind, and right now, she was sure he knew she had been miles away.

Madame Butterfly always had the power to take her back to the mini-sabbatical she had in New York and the performance she saw at the Metropolitan Opera in the Lincoln Center.

The auditorium combines old-world elegance with sleek contemporary, with around 3,800 seats and 245 standing-room positions. The acoustic is superb.

Grandiose.

· · ·

For Gabrielle, though, the Met is just too big. Instead, she prefers the Royal Opera House in London, with 2,256 odd seats offering a far more intimate experience.

Like New York - London. The VP and Mr Wonderful.

Madame Butterfly with the VP was a show, an occasion to get dressed, socialise and be seen.

   With Mr Wonderful was a moment to cherish if she could only stop being dragged back.

Is the past ever gone? Memories intruded the present moment, fantasies dropping into the continuous present of our lives.

Everything is always present. Vivid imagining sometimes feels more real than reality itself.

   How easy to be confused.

The New York trip kept popping in her mind, intruding.

A last-minute decision after a long-term relationship break-up. She needed to escape, an adventure, re-group and re-think what she would do.

On her taxi ride from the airport, she felt like a mini Indiana Jones on her first-ever trip alone, non-work-related. Not visiting anybody. Nothing planned. Just her and New York. Exhilarating and scary AF.

She had decided to go for three months, longer than the usual holiday but short enough not to need a working visa.

It seemed like a good idea at the time.

By the second month there, the novelty was wearing thin without a job or friends to meet and the VP at work during the day.

Gabrielle had walked Manhattan from top to bottom and east to west. She had almost memorised every street.

Well, it certainly felt like it.

She had met the VP on her first day there, and they had been going out ever since. He had taken her to all his haunts and introduced her to all the right people (HIS right people)

—the perfect chaperon with benefits.

She was bored.

Holidays are relatively short periods that one plans. This New York trip had been unexpected, totally unplanned and without any schedule, and Gabrielle was always used to having something occupying her mind, side by side with a very active social life.

· · ·

She was so bored that she started watching television far more than she was used to back home, flicking from channel to channel (far too many).

She often settled for the Law and Order franchise, something familiar to watch, always a fan of murder mysteries and crime dramas. Gabrielle was particularly fond of Law and Order Criminal Intent and one of its characters: Detective Robert Goren, played brilliantly by character actor Vincent D'Onofrio.

Detective Goren was tall, dark and handsome, moody and incredibly perceptive in a Sherlockesque deducing manner.
     He also is totally screwed up in his relationships.

In other words: perfect and her usual type.

To pass her time, she started googling to find out where they were filming, if any filming was going on, and which actor was filming.
     She considered going too.

Reddit seemed the place to find out together with every possible D'Onofrio/Goren sighting, the two more and more intertwined in Gabrielle's mind. An intelligent and attractive hero, right here in New York. Where she was right now.

She was almost living a double life.
     By night living the sparkling NY City life with the VP.

By day searching the internet for the latest place where Goren had been seen:

- Bond St,
- Stuyvesant Town,
- Bleecker Street ...

One day, she read that he was a regular in Tompkins Square Park, Christodora House, so she walked down from MidTown and stayed there for hours.

H-O-U-R-S.

Waiting.

Nothing happened, of course, besides that she had turned into a semi-stalker.

Then, on her way back to the TownePlace, she saw him. Right at the intersection of Third Avenue and 14th Street.

Goren was driving a big dark Range Rover.

Ok, no clue what car it was, a big one. Her heart was beating fast. She actually saw him. Live.

And, just like that, he was gone. Just like that, she had turned into an obsessed teenage stalker.

Splendid.

God knows what she thought she would do had she properly met him. Fall madly in love and move permanently to New York. Or him moving to London? She hadn't thought that far.

She was just searching for something and not finding it. She hated to admit that she was always going for emotionally or physically unavailable men.

What if she was always choosing people who don't allow intimacy? Was it because, deep down, she didn't want it?

Or was she afraid she'd lose herself entirely if she let herself be loved?
    Was SHE the one afraid?

How could she stop hooking up with emotionally unavailable people? People who can't actually love her.

And now, here she was, with Mr Wonderful.

Right here, right now, the most physically and emotionally available man she had ever met.
    Totally devoted to her.

· · ·

She could see a common denominator when she looked back at her quasi-relationships that didn't work out.

Herself.

The Working-Class Millionaire who worked very hard for his money. And the more he earned, the harder he had to work to balance out his low inner worth set point.

"He is a m-i-l-l-i-o-n-a-i-r-e" his mouth filling up.
    One of the very first things he ever told her.

He was constantly trying to surpass his father, a working-class immigrant who made a fortune post-war but he never believed he could.

She never understood how an investment banker had such an aversion to money and being wealthy.

Truth be told, he had never quite adapted to his new habitat.

But, on the other hand, Gabrielle was always striving to improve, and that attitude was inconceivable to her - she had left her village behind,
    both mentally and physically.

. . .

She couldn't quite understand how one would want to remain a moth instead of becoming a butterfly.

The Stud was tall and muscular with deep green eyes, voluptuous lips, and a voracious sexual appetite.

The fact that he was several years younger than she made it even more exciting, talking about men-in-power-with younger totty in tow.

Except for this time, she was the one in power, for a change, and the man was the totty.

The thrill, coupled with the validation, was a potent aphrodisiac. And at the beginning, it was fun and exciting, but after a while, it became tedious; she wanted a proper relationship, not every weekend alone.

And even though all the signs were there, she ignored them.

He was a cancer survivor in remission who used his cancer as his Linus blanket.

Gabrielle had thought of leaving him so many times, and the sob story would come out each time.

・ ・ ・

She had fallen for someone with so many red flags that he could have been an air traffic controller. But, giving him the benefit of the doubt, she continued to see him.

She didn't want to be the heartless cow that went him when he was down in the dumps, depressed.

Six months after they finally split, she came across a charity website and there it was: a picture of a couple who had a very successful fundraising event -

The Stud and his girlfriend.

The problem was that the fundraising event took place when they were still together. Gabrielle had been THE OTHER WOMAN.

Then came the QC. The famous QC.

Smart, attractive, with his life, totally figured out. And someone with bigger balls than hers.

But, perhaps, in insight, they were too big.

The QC was brilliant, and Gabrielle enjoyed their long debates, proud he was comfortable talking about his cases and asked her opinion.

. . .

His mind was absolutely mesmerising. His ego was equally ginormous. A man used to live life on his terms with people around him accommodating every single one of his whims.

That's how Gabriele liked it too. It was unbearable mainly because it was like looking in a mirror and not quite liking what you see.

The Champagne Socialist followed. Another mirror but, this time, not liking that much what you see. Perfection is so hard to achieve, and trying to be perfect all the time is exhausting.
  Perfectionitis is a terrible disease.

Always striving, never arriving.

Gabrielle had kept looking, convinced that she'd find someone who wanted to be with her because she was *special*.

Like the Champagne Socialist: working-class, uber gifted, scholarship for Eton, EVP in one of the Big 4 consulting firms, and still suffering from Impostor Syndrome.

They were the same man. They were HER. Gabrielle was afraid of getting hurt. It was not them.
  It was her.

Truly opening up to someone and having them reciprocate is an intimate bond. What if the relationship fails?

. . .

They were perfect and the safe option. Since they were guarding their emotions closely, there was a decreased risk of emotional engagement. A.K.A. getting hurt.

Gabrielle couldn't deny that the thrill of the dating chase was fun.

Wanting what you cannot have it's a never-ending, dead-end chase with intermittent positive reinforcement. Up and down. Reward and withdrawal.

Committed to not committing.

And in New York, she was living a fantasy in her head that didn't require putting in an effort to make an *actual* relationship work.

So the VP was the holiday fling and Goren, Goren, was the ultimate emotionally unavailable person, someone she "couldn't have" because he didn't actually exist.

A television character brilliantly interpreted. That's all.

And now this fantastic man was in her life, and she couldn't find any faults. He was present and engaging in a more profound, authentic and emotional way. Mr Wonderful had never made any promises that he hadn't kept. He was there, fully, completely, emotionally and physically available.

Ed egli alquanto in pena
Chiamerà, chiamerà
"Piccina, mogliettina
Olezzo di verbena"
I nomi che mi dava al suo venire
Tutto questo avverrà, te lo prometto
Tienti la tua paura
Io con sicura fede l'aspetto

As the heartbreaking song was coming to an end, a tear started rushing down her cheek.

"It's ok", he said, "it's ok .
    Io sono qui, e ti aspetto,"

AFTERWORD

Consciousness itself creates the material world. The linear passing of time in stark contrast with the seemingly random crossing of time in our consciousness.

And the stream is constant.

Everything is NOW. And memories provide a constant connection to events, places and people.

There are infinite possibilities that the world can offer at every moment .

Choose wisely.

Laura xxx

DISCLAIMER

A Searching for Goren is a work of fiction.

Although its form is that of a recollected autobiography, it is not one.

With the exception of public places any resemblance to persons living or dead is coincidental. Space and time have been rearranged to suit the convenience of the book, memory has its own story to tell.

The opinions expressed are those of the characters and should not be confused with the author's.

AUTHOR'S NOTE

Thank you so much for reading *Searching for Goren.*

I hope you enjoyed this novella as an escapist story, but perhaps you also glimpsed something beneath as you read. A review would be much appreciated as it helps other readers discover the story. Thanks.

If you sign up for my newsletter you'll be notified of giveaways, new releases and receive personal updates from behind the scenes of my business and books.

Go to www.thepeoplealchemist.com to get started.

Places in the book

I have set the story in real places in New York and at a time in the past which might not be still operational.

You can see some of the places here:

- Royal Opera House, London
- The Metropolitan Opera, New York
- Times Square
- TownePlace Suites, Manhattan / Times Square

- NYC West Village

Bibliography

I read a lot of books as part of my research. Some of them together with other references include:

Psycho-Cybernetics - **Maxwell Maltz**
The Complete Reader - **Neville Goddard**

Law and Order : Criminal Intent - American crime drama television, third series in Dick Wolf's successful Law and Order franchise. Detective Robert Goren is one of the main original character played by actor Vincent D'Onofrio, a modern tortured but brilliant Sherlock Holmes like figure.

Printed in Great Britain
by Amazon